Tabitha Fink

The Cat With One Eye

by Rick Felty

tabithafink.com

hi

ISBN-13 978-0989912822
ISBN-10 0989912825

Printed in the United States of America

Published by Dreamschooner Press.

www.dreamschoonerpress.com

For Keaton, who named our cat in one magically inspired moment. Kylie who gave all our pets a chance to make themselves at home. Geo, who helped me feel the magic of children's books. Dorie, who kept the dream alive for too many years and Tabitha Fink, who found her way to us.

A portion of the proceeds from the sale of this book
will be donated to Young Storytellers.

Young Storytellers sparks creative self-discovery through storytelling.
Their programs highlight young people
as the center of their own narratives,
emphasize that their stories matter,
and celebrate their unique voices as the ones telling them.

I am Tabitha Fink

quite simply a cat.

Not a car

or a star

or a bear
with a hat.

Not
a
boat

or a truck

or a ball
and a bat.

I am Tabitha Fink

and that truly is that.

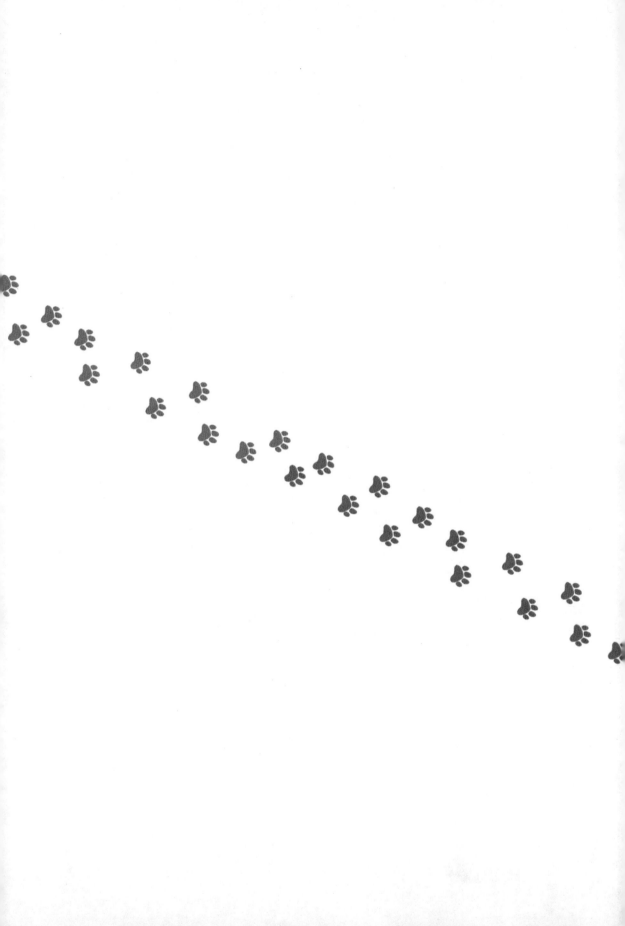

I am Tabitha Fink,

a cat
with
one eye.

Not a doll

or a train

or a kite

that can fly.

14

Not a hammer

or shovel

or blueberry pie.

I am Tabitha Fink

and
I love
my
one eye.

I am Tabitha Fink,
somewhat hard
to ignore

with only
one eye

where
some others
have more.

I've still got
one tail

and four paws
on the floor.

I'm still Tabitha Fink

as I've
mentioned before.

Because I have
one

where
sometimes
there are
two,

and because when
you look

I seem different
to you.

it makes me
more special
with each single
blink.

I am happy as me.

I am Tabitha Fink.

So if you're a cow

with blue
spots on her back,

or a duck that goes

"beep beep"

"snort snort"

and not quack,

don't worry yourself

what some others
might think.

You're great

as you are,

just like
Tabitha Fink.

bye

Rick Felty lives in New England
with his wonderful family and lots of pets.

Visit
tabithafink.com

to get a free audio book version of
"Tabitha Fink: The Cat With One Eye"
with extra content!

AND you can see a picture of the real Tabitha Fink
and learn more about why she only has one eye.

Also available in the Award-Winning Tabitha Fink Series

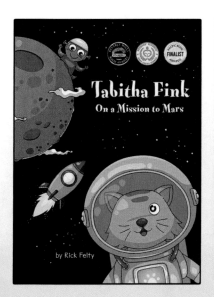

Made in the USA
Las Vegas, NV
15 December 2024

14234671R00029